Galia Bernstein

The Pumpernickel-Daffodil

to Milo
You are best in show!
xx

Abrams Books for Young Readers · New York

Wodehouse Chili Pepper Pumpernickel the Third
has an important family.

His mother is the famous
Mathilda Lily-Rose Daffodil.

And his father is the celebrated
Wodehouse Chili Pepper
Pumpernickel the Second.

It's a family of champions,
blue-ribbon winners,
and Bests in Show galore . . .

and all of them agree that one day,
he will be the best of them all!

After all, he IS a Pumpernickel-Daffodil.

"Darling," said Mother one day,
"it's time for you to get your own human."

"Why do I need a human?"

"Well, when you trot around the ring in a dog show,"
said Father, "looking MAGNIFICENT,
a human in a suit is trotting beside you,
looking very silly indeed."

"You can't win ribbons without one,"
said Mother. "Don't ask me why."

"But how do I get a human?"

"They will come to you," said Mother.
"You just sit up straight and look bored.
That's how people know you're important.
Now, let's practice. Can you sit up for Mommy?
That's a good boy!"

Isadora Alexandra Ball's people are dog people.

Her father is a dog groomer.
The BEST dog groomer!

Her mother shows dogs.
Her mother's mother shows dogs.

When Isadora was eight years old,
they all agreed it was time for her
to get a show dog of her own.

Wodehouse Chili Pepper Pumpernickel the Third sat in a little room, on a little bed, by a little sign with his big name on it, trying to look bored.

Wodehouse
Chili Pepper
Pumpernickel III

SIRE: Wodehouse Chili
Pepper Pumpernickel II

DAM: Mathilda
Lily-Rose Daffodil

It was easy because he WAS bored.
And sleepy . . .

When he woke up, a girl was standing there staring at him.

He yawned . . .

Oh no! He's not supposed to yawn!

He sat up straight . . .
Oh no! His ear
was inside out!

Shake to the right—

didn't work.

Shake to the left—

worked!

He sat up straight again.
The girl giggled.
"This one, Mom!"

"I don't know . . ." said her mom.
"He's a bit scrawny, he's a bit scruffy, he's a . . ."
 She bent down to read the sign.

"PUMPERNICKEL-DAFFODIL??? We'll take him!"

"I'm Isadora Alexandra Ball," said the girl on the way home,
"but you can call me Izzy. You are . . ." she looked at the note in her hand.

"Wode . . . house? Chili Pepper
Pumpa-what? Can I call you Chili?"

Chili wagged his tail.
The name felt just right.

"Time for training!"
said Izzy's mom a few days later.
"You both have a lot to learn
about how to behave in dog shows."

Sit like this.

Not like that.

Stand like this.

Not like that.

Run like this.

Not like . . .

"IZZY!"

"Time for a bath and a haircut!"
said Izzy's dad the day before the show.

"Yes, Chili," said Izzy.
"Time for your bath and haircut."

"I meant both of you," said Dad.

NEVER!!!!!! yelled Izzy as she ran out of the room.

So they had a bath

and a haircut

and . . .

"We look silly," said Izzy.
"Why are my shoes so shiny?"

Chili just stared.

He was fluffy.

He was poofy.

He was . . .

HALF NAKED!

But there was no going back now . . .

"And . . . we're back! At the Junior Dog Show, I'm Helen Rashbone."

"And I'm Diego de los Perros. Who's next, Helen?"

"Next is Isadora Alexandra Ball
and Wodehouse Chili Pepper,
who is a Pumpernickel-Daffodil!"

"He is on the podium,
that's a perfect stance . . .

and now they are running around the ring,

but—oh no! Isadora lost a shoe!"

"Look, Helen! The dog has
the shoe in his mouth!"

"Aww, he is trying to put
the shoe back on her foot.
Like a little Prince Charming . . .

Diego, the shoe is back on,
and they are off . . .
in the wrong direction.

The crowd is chanting

WRONG WAY!

and they are . . .

running backward?"

"And now they're . . .
Are they dancing, Helen?
And the crowd is on their feet!"

"Oops," giggled Izzy as they
danced backward out of the ring.
"I don't think we're getting a ribbon."

"Oh, dear," said Izzy's mom backstage.
"My daughter, the dog show comedian.
What will my mother say?
And her mother?"

"They would say that we have
an amazing little girl!" said Dad.

They were all smiling,
and Chili was happy,
but uh-oh!
His own parents
were coming over.

"That was . . . different," said Mother.

"She was laughing too," said Father.

"Well, I can't help it if my boy is funny,"
said Mother with a huff.
"He gets it from my side of the family.
The Daffodils are ALL famous wits."

"Nonsense," said Father.
"The Pumpernickels are known to be HILARIOUS!"

"I'm sorry," said Chili.

"For what, dear?" said Mother.

"For not behaving like a Pumpernickel-Daffodil."

"How would we know what a
Pumpernickel-Daffodil behaves like?"
said Father. "You are the only one.
The one and only
Wodehouse Chili Pepper
Pumpernickel-Daffodil!"

"Call me Chili," said Chili.

"Yes, dear."

To Oliver,
A good boy.
And to my mom and dad,
Good parents.

The art for this book was created digitally
with applied hand-painted textures.

Cataloging-in-Publication Data has been applied for
and may be obtained from the Library of Congress.

ISBN 978-1-4197-5945-1

Text and illustrations © 2023 Galia Bernstein
Book design by Natalie Padberg Bartoo

Published in 2023 by Abrams Books for Young Readers, an imprint of
ABRAMS. All rights reserved. No portion of this book may be reproduced,
stored in a retrieval system, or transmitted in any form or by any means,
mechanical, electronic, photocopying, recording, or otherwise,
without written permission from the publisher.

Printed and bound in China
10 9 8 7 6 5 4 3 2 1

Abrams Books for Young Readers are available at special discounts when
purchased in quantity for premiums and promotions as well as fundraising
or educational use. Special editions can also be created to specification. For
details, contact specialsales@abramsbooks.com or the address below.

Abrams® is a registered trademark of Harry N. Abrams, Inc.

ABRAMS The Art of Books
195 Broadway, New York, NY 10007
abramsbooks.com